Little Red
Robin

Do you have all the Little Red Robin books?

- [ ] Buster's Big Surprise
- [ ] The Purple Butterfly
- [ ] How Bobby Got His Pet
- [ ] We are Super!
- [ ] New Friends
- [ ] Robo-Robbie

Also available as ebooks

If you feel ready to read a longer book,
look out for more stories about Willow Valley

Little Red
Robin

New Friends

Tracey Corderoy
Illustrated by Hannah Whitty

■SCHOLASTIC

For Charlotte, with all my love. . .

T.C xx

Scholastic Children's Books
An imprint of Scholastic Ltd.
Euston House, 24 Eversholt Street
London, NW1 1DB, UK
Registered office: Westfield Road, Southam, Warwickshire, CV47 0RA
SCHOLASTIC and associated logos are trademarks and/or registered
trademarks of Scholastic Inc.

First published in the UK in 2014 by Scholastic Ltd

Text copyright © Tracey Corderoy, 2014
Illustrations © Hannah Whitty, 2014

The rights of Tracey Corderoy and Hannah Whitty
to be identified as the author and illustrator of
this work have been asserted by them.

ISBN 978 1407 138855

A CIP catalogue record for this book is available from the British Library

Riley, a little toffee-coloured mouse, was outside in his new garden. He had only just moved to Willow Valley, but he loved his garden already! It had tall, swishy grass and lots of places that were just right for making a den. But first he needed to finish off his new go-kart.

Riley fixed on the last wheel. "Hooray!" he cheered. It was done! A big bright smile spread from whisker to whisker.

Just then, Riley's mum came out with the washing. A tiny, fluffy white mouse was riding in the basket, on top of the wet towels. Mimi-Rose, Riley's little sister, loved washing-day rides!

"Look, Mum," called Riley. He showed her his go-kart.

"Very smart," his mother smiled.

She put down her basket and knelt beside
Riley. "Can you pop to the village square?" she
asked. "We need some cakes from the bakers."

"Oh, yes!" squeaked Riley. "I'll drive there in
my new go-kart!"

Riley's mum gave him some money for the cakes. Then she checked he knew the way.

"It's just down the hill, remember?" she said.

"I know!" giggled Riley. They had walked there just yesterday. But maybe today he'd meet some children. Riley really wanted to make some new friends soon. . .

Riley jumped into his go-kart and set off down the hill. His long whiskers were blowing out behind him.

"Wheee!" he giggled as he flew through the grass, sending daisy petals everywhere. His little go-kart went like the wind. "Wow!"

As Riley reached the bottom of the hill he tried to stop the go-kart. He pulled the brake lever hard. Then . . . *snap!*

Riley looked down. The brakes had broken. "Oh no!" he said with a gasp.

The go-kart flew into the village square – over the grass, through the neat flower beds, up the pavements and down. Everyone jumped out of the way.

"Beep beep!" shouted Riley. "I can't stop!"

Finally, with a crash, the go-kart hit a tree.

Riley tumbled through the air and landed in a bush.

"Bother!" he said crossly.

As he wriggled out he heard the patter of paws.
Then a fluffy-faced badger suddenly appeared.
She had a daisy in her hair.

"Are you OK?" the badger asked Riley.

"Yes," sighed Riley. "I'm all right, but I'm not so sure about my go-kart."

The go-kart was lying upside down on the grass, underneath the tree. Riley and the badger went over to see it.

"The brakes have broken," Riley explained. He showed the badger how the lever had snapped off.

"You definitely need brakes around here," the badger said. "The hills are so steep."

The badger smiled at Riley. "I can help you fix them if you want me to…" she offered.

"Yes, please," squeaked Riley, nodding his head. "Thanks!"

"My name is Starla," said the badger. "Nice to meet you."

"Nice to meet you too!" replied Riley. "I'm Riley. I've just moved to Willow Valley."

"Well, in that case, let me show you around!" smiled Starla.

Starla led Riley around the village square. In the middle of it was a giant tree which looked like it nearly touched the sky!

"At Christmas," said Starla, "we put a star on the top. And we all have roast chestnuts, too."

"Wow," said Riley. That sounded like so much fun!

Then Starla showed him the Library Cave.
"It has all kinds of stories," she said. "You can
take books home as well."

"Even explorer books?" Riley asked. Those
were his favourite.

Starla nodded. She said there were books
about everything.

Next, they passed the village school. "Hey, there's a tree swing," Riley grinned. He loved swings!

When they reached the toy shop window, Riley gave an excited squeak. "This is my grandpa's shop," he said. "We moved here to live near Grandpa."

"I got my rocking-horse from your grandpa's shop," Starla told him.

The next shop along was the baker's. There were
all kinds of cakes in the window. There were jam
tarts, and ginger cake, and big sticky buns.

"And look at those ones," Starla said. She pointed to a plate of fairy cakes with icing and cherries on the top.

"Mmmm," said Riley, licking his lips. He'd never seen so many yummy-looking cakes before!

Starla took Riley down to the river. She wanted to show him the boats. Three long boats bobbed about on the water.

"That's my grandpa's boat," said Starla, pointing to the pale blue boat with a kingfisher painted on the front. "Maybe Grandpa will let you ride in it one day."

"Really?" gasped Riley. "That would be amazing!"

Riley saw that the boat had a long, thick rope which dangled down into the water. His toy boat had a rope like this too, with a big shiny anchor on the end.

Suddenly, Riley remembered something. Anchors made boats stop still! And then he had a really good idea. . .

"My go-kart!" cried Riley. "We could make an anchor-brake. That wouldn't snap like the wooden one did!" The problem was, what could they use to make it?

Riley and Starla thought very hard.

"I know!" cried Starla.

"What?" asked Riley. It was great having someone to plan with!

"I've got just the thing," Starla grinned. "Wait there!"

Starla pattered on to her grandpa's boat and came back with a shiny wire coat hanger.

Then they bent it into an anchor shape together.

They tied the new anchor-brake on to the
go-kart. But now they had to test it out. "Ooooh!"
said Starla excitedly. "Come with me!"

She grabbed Riley's paw and whisked him off
to a really good hill nearby. Riley wanted to climb
to the very top, so Starla helped him carry the
go-kart up.

When they got there, Riley got the go-kart
ready. "OK!" he squeaked. He was about to jump
in when. . .

"Wait!" cried Starla. "We're up too high. If the
brake doesn't work you'll crash again. Maybe we
should try it further down the hill?"

They hurried back down.
Then Riley jumped in the
go-kart and it rolled down
the gentle slope.

When he wanted the
go-kart to stop he
dropped the anchor
over the side. But the
ground was too hard
and it wouldn't stick in.

Then the anchor
bounced against a
rock and got bent.

"First snapping brakes and now bent ones!"
Riley groaned.

The kart trundled on and finally stopped when
it reached some tall, thick grass. Riley shook his
head and sighed.

"What now, then?" asked Starla. "Shall we try something else?"

"I know!" said a big, boomy voice. They looked around, but no one was there.

Then down through the sky came the funniest
sight. . .

A parachuting hedgehog!

"Woo hoo!" hooted the roly-poly hedgehog as it
landed in the daisies with a bump!

"That's Horatio Spark," giggled Starla. "He's my friend and he's really, really funny!"

They helped untangle Horatio from his parachute, which was really just a sheet off his bed.

Then Riley wheeled the go-kart over.

"Did you say you knew what to do?" he asked.

"Yep, easy-peasy!" Horatio grinned. "I always use a parachute-brake on my go-karts!"

Horatio bundled up his bedsheet and held it out to Riley. "Try this!" he said. Then he and Starla helped Riley tie it on to the go-kart.

They pulled the kart halfway up the hill.
"Ready for a ride, then?" Riley smiled.

"You'd like us to ride with you?" Starla asked.

"Sure!" Riley nodded. "You did help me out.
Come on!"

On the count of three they jumped into the go-kart and it flew off down the hill.

"Wheee!" cried Riley. It went even faster with two new friends on board!

When it was time to stop, Horatio tossed the parachute high into the air. The wind caught it at once, and it puffed up like a big white balloon!

"Wow!" beamed Riley, as the go-kart slowed down. "We did it! We did it!"

"Hooray!" cheered everyone.

They played and played. It was so much fun.
They zipped, and they zoomed, and their whiskers
blew out behind them!

It was only when Horatio's tummy rumbled
loudly that Riley remembered something. . .

"Ooops! I was meant to buy cakes," he said.
He'd been having so much fun he'd forgotten!

"Can we come too?" Starla asked.

"I love cake," said Horatio.

"OK!" Riley nodded. "Let's go!"

They drove all the way to the village square,
where Riley's mum was looking for him.

"Oh, Riley – there you are!" she smiled, and
Mimi-Rose hugged him tightly.

"Mum, these are my new friends," said Riley,
"Starla and Horatio."

Riley's mum gave them both a big smile, too.
"Pleased to meet you!"

Everyone followed
Riley into the baker's
where he bought a big
ginger cake to share.

"Mmmm," said
Horatio, licking his
lips. "My favourite!"

As they ate it
under a giant
tree, Riley had
never felt happier.
He had cake *and*
a go-kart. . .

But best of all, he had two new friends.

"I'm going to love living in Willow Valley," he said with a big fluffy smile. Then he quickly helped himself to more cake, before a roly-poly hedgehog scoffed the lot!